Emily
via the Greyhound Bus

EMILY

VIA THE GREYHOUND BUS

ALLISON KYDD

thistledown press

Thistledown Press Ltd.
118 - 20th Street West
Saskatoon, Saskatchewan, S7M 0W6
www.thistledownpress.com

Library and Archives Canada Cataloguing in Publication

Kydd, Allison
Emily via the Greyhound bus / Allison Kydd.

Short stories.
ISBN 978-1-927068-09-0

I. Title.

PS8621.Y43E65 2012   C813'.6   C2012-904723-6

An early version of *Emily via the Greyhound Bus* was serialized in *Our Voice,* Edmonton's spare-change newspaper.

Cover and book design by Jackie Forrie
Printed and bound in Canada

 Canada Council Conseil des Arts
for the Arts du Canada

 SASKATCHEWAN
ARTS BOARD

 Canadian Patrimoine
Heritage canadien

Thistledown Press gratefully acknowledges the financial assistance of the Canada Council for the Arts, the Saskatchewan Arts Board, and the Government of Canada through the Canada Book Fund for its publishing program.

Acknowledgements

This slender volume must carry the weight of many thanks: for the love and support of my partner, Kevin Whittingham, and of my children, Joy, Niko, and Bobby Yiannakoulias; for the encouragement of my sisters and brothers and our mother, Joyce Kydd, who taught us, and our late father, William Donald Kydd, who always believed in us.

It's also a delight to thank many writer friends and mentors, among them Alistair MacLeod, Myrna Garanis, Betty Jane Hegerat, Audrey Whitson, Astrid Blodgett, Mary Dawe, Shirley Serviss, and other loyal bookish friends too numerous to mention — for their unwavering patience.

Thanks are also due to Welby Walker and Kevin Whittingham, my referees for the original Anvil Press submission; as well as to editors and mentors Keith Wiley, former editor of *Our Voice*, Edmonton's spare-change newspaper, for his trust that I would send him an installment every month; Dave Margoshes and Larry Pratt, for their early insights about this manuscript; and especially Susan Musgrave, for her kindness and meticulous attention to detail when reading the final drafts.

I'm also grateful to the Writers' Guild of Alberta (WGA) and the Saskatchewan Writers' Guild (SWG) for their retreat programs, as I would have written much less over the years without the space provided by St. Peter's Abbey, Banff Centre, and Rudy and Tena Wiebe's Strawberry Creek Lodge. Since writers, the SWG and the WGA are also supported by the Saskatchewan Arts Board and the Alberta Foundation for the Arts, those programs also deserve tremendous thanks.

Finally, I thank Thistledown Press, and Al and Jackie Forrie for their trust and encouragement and for persisting with the New Leaf Editions in these times of uncertainty and spectacular change.

This book of fiction is dedicated to three dear friends whom I no longer see: Lois Hogarth, Marlene Lerat and Donna Cheechoo. Who knows where stories begin!

Contents

Introducing Emily

EMILY STAGGERED DOWN THE AISLE BETWEEN the two rows of seats. She made it to the toilet just in time, managing to shut the door behind her before she puked on the painted toilet seat and metal bench.

When her stomach stopped heaving, she sank into a squat in the space between wall and door. That stopped the trembling in her knees but not the refrain in her head.

Help me — Jeremy, help me.

Though she'd walked out on him, she hated being alone and knew the ache would get worse before it got better.

When Emily could stand and raise her eyes from the slush on the bench to the mirror wall behind, she caught her reflection and was surprised to see no change. Her skin was green-tinged from the dim light in the cubicle, and the camouflage T-shirt stretched across her breasts looked grey. Other than that, one would never know.

The same heart-shaped face, the same prominent cheekbones and high forehead, the same curtain of dark hair, still untouched by grey. The girls at the convent school had admired her hair. They wished *they* were Indian, they said. Even her *kookum* had told her she was pretty, that her mom had the same eyes. "Shaped like almonds," Kookum had said, "same long eyelashes too, and pouty mouth."

Yet Emily's mom had seen hard times since she was a girl, and her face had changed.

Staring at her reflection, Emily noticed her lips gaping in what Marty had called her "Lolita" look. *Marty.* She hadn't understood the reference but knew from his tone it couldn't be good.

She tasted another spasm. When it subsided, she considered how to clean up the mess. Luckily, it was morning. The bus had just been serviced, and the paper towel dispenser was full, though she found no little foil packages with their antiseptic scent to cover the smell.

Someone rattled the door latch, and Emily whacked a response with the flat of her hand. The smack hurt — good clean pain shot up her palm and across her wrist. She squared her shoulders and got to work.

At first the towels came from the dispenser in pieces. When she was finally able to wrangle out larger chunks, she scraped the still-warm vomit into the toilet hole.

"Do Not Deposit Paper Towels or Other Foreign Objects in Toilet" said the sign. And over the garbage flap: "Deposit Paper Towels Here."

Screw them.

She imagined some rich chick getting a surprise while stuffing her towel into the bin like the sign said, and almost laughed aloud.

Of course, a rich chick wouldn't be travelling Greyhound, while Emily had no choice. She also cleaned up her own messes — or it didn't get done. That was being a grown-up.

If only Jeremy could see her now! Come to think of it, she'd never seen Jeremy with a mess to clear up. Too much class — same as Marty. Yet both had called her "needy," when she'd fended for herself since she was seventeen. What did they know about it? How dared they think so little of her!

The sisters too should see her now. They'd taught her something about being self-reliant. If there'd only been more kindness to go with the rules, she'd have better memories of the place.

She wrenched herself back to the present. When had she last thrown up like this? Best she couldn't remember — hadn't been that drunk for a long time. Jeremy had kept her on the straight and narrow.

She hadn't even thrown up when she was pregnant, though just a kid herself the first time — long before Jeremy, or even Marty. The other sickness was nothing to do with drinking or what she ate, just a constant yearning inside her. Jeremy couldn't understand. He thought she always had a choice.

Men — always there until you needed them, and then . . .

Again, Emily almost laughed — this time through tears. As she braced herself against the roll and sway of the bus, her belly churned again. No wonder, with the smell of piss and puke and the sound of sloshing liquid under the toilet seat.

As always when sick or in pain, she longed for her mom, for the comfort of her hands and just the scent of her. It had been worth being sick, staying home from school, having Mom's full attention and Kookum offering hot soup and bannock.

Like the time she sprained her ankle and the gym teacher carried her to the school bus. Even after her ankle was better, she remembered the touch of his large hands as he lifted her so easily, the ripple of his shoulder against her forehead when she hid her face, how he told her to put her arms around his neck. In fact, she was never able to look him in the face again.

Mr. Forester, the school bus driver, drove them all the way home, with seven-year-old Teresa in the front seat telling him the way. Emily and her sisters were the only reserve kids on the bus, and another time she'd have been embarrassed to have the others see where she lived. This time she hardly minded their curious faces pressed against the window. Everyone had been very kind, and the bus took the bumpy dirt track right to the door of her mom's house.

And Mom and Kookum and the little ones came rushing out to see what had happened. Mom had rollers in her hair and was wearing her baggy sweater and those patched jeans she cinched around her waist with safety pins and string, yet Emily hardly cared.

When they saw Emily wasn't hurt too bad, Mom and Kookum invited the driver and all the kids to stay for supper. Mr. Forester seemed impressed by their easy hospitality.

"No, thank you," he said politely — they all had folks waiting for them.

When the bus left, Kookum went looking for witch hazel, marsh mallow, and other roots. These she boiled until soft enough for a poultice, using strips of cloth from one of Emily's dad's old shirts to hold it secure around Emily's ankle. Though the swelling was gone after a few days, Emily's mom and kookum continued to fuss over her. They scolded her for hopping around the kitchen bumping into the furniture instead of staying in bed or lying on the chesterfield.

All long gone.

Another spasm. Emily pulled her hair back from her face, lifted the toilet cover, and aimed at the black, sloshing hole in the middle of the bench.

More rattling of the door handle, a man's voice harsh against the doorjamb: "You died in there?"

Screw you.

Most men were either jerks or heartbreakers, and there was no doubt about this one. His voice again — "Sure you ain't died?" Some joker!

I'm thinkin' 'bout it.

Emily via the Greyhound Bus

She finished cleaning up, even used fresh towels to rewipe all the surfaces. The place still stank of vomit — nothing more she could do about that — and her mouth tasted foul. But another "Please Do Not" sign warned her against drinking the water.

As she emerged from the toilet, she raised an eyebrow at the man who'd been waiting. "Believe me, I did you a favour."

He scowled at her breasts, which she knew were outlined in dark perspiration through her thin shirt. "Huh?" He took a whiff through the open door. "You're kidding," and pretended to gag.

May your takây *shrivel up and die.*

She gave back gaze for gaze. Wilted shirt over grubby T-shirt, fringe of sandy hair bordering his Adam's apple. Tooled-leather belt spanning a belly that tested his shirt buttons, jeans riding pitifully low and legs too skinny for the rest of him.

Martin Feldstein Jr. — Marty for short — had fretted about weight. Emily never knew why; he always looked good to her. Perhaps because his idol Humphrey Bogart was lean as a greyhound — no extra flesh on him. Emily hadn't understood the hero worship either, especially of such an old geezer.

She headed back to the seat she had abandoned twenty minutes before. *You asshole,* said her shoulders, her slender arms, the female sway of her hips, as she left the man at the back of the bus. *Eat your heart out.*

The heater was going full blast, so she pulled her heavy leather coat around her for comfort not for warmth.

Woman Alone

THE SURGE OF POWER EMILY HAD experienced outside the washroom faded quickly when Marty came to mind. He had hurt her the most — she understood now, when it mattered less.

When she'd met him, she didn't recognize the danger. He had the air of a man who was going places. Insecure people put on cool. Not Marty. He was clean, polite, eager, and irresistible.

How long ago had it been? Ten years? Fifteen? People had these all-night binges in the sixties — crowded rooms, bead curtains, incense and candles on the windowsills, pot in the living room, and their own Yankee draft dodger sleeping in the basement when he didn't get a better offer.

Before Marty appeared with his expensive loafers and college-boy good looks and settled down so close Emily felt the heat of his body, she hadn't intended to stay. She often melted back into the crowds as if she were invisible. Instead, she watched him fold his tweed sports jacket across his lap, cross his legs, rest elbows on knees and chin on hands. His beard was patchy, obviously new, and his jeans weren't from any local store. She wondered how he came to be there — could have been a cop, except party people kept a sharp eye out for cops.

When Marty told her his name, his dark eyes and quizzical smile made Emily flush, so she was disappointed when he closed his eyes to tune into the sitar music from the record player in the corner and seemed to forget her. When he dropped the weed, however, burning a tiny hole in his new-looking jeans, she didn't think less of him.

Though she drank, Emily didn't do drugs, not even marijuana; she wasn't into trusting people that much. So she passed the toke along without taking a turn. Then she leaned closer to Marty, felt his arm rub her breast through the thin fabric of her shirt. Noticed him shifting his position to get more of the feel of her.

It wouldn't be the first time she'd hooked up at a party, taken home somebody she'd just met, spent the night screwing. Some guys were okay, although such encounters never turned into anything permanent. She thought she liked it that way.

She had her own place and a job as a receptionist. Before that she was either a cocktail waitress or a hostess, usually in good establishments. She'd also been a short-order cook, desk clerk at a small hotel, and a gas jockey. Like her friends and lovers, her jobs were temporary, and that too was okay. If a boss got fresh or co-workers turned mean, she'd move on once she had enough to pay her bills. Since the school, nobody had paid much attention to what she did and where she went, and the school felt like a long time ago.

"Excuse me, miss."

"Wha . . . " She jerked upright when the hand landed on her shoulder. Stared at the faded make-up bag dangling from the man's fist.

"You left it in the can when . . . you know."

"Oh, thanks." Emily took the bag between thumb and forefinger. God knows why he'd kept it all this time. Checked out the contents for sure. Good thing there was nothing important inside. She'd stopped using the pill a while back because Jeremy worried about side effects.

"You must of partied hard last night."

Emily didn't answer. Bet he wouldn't talk to a white chick like that.

"Had a hard time finding you. You hiding or something?"

Get lost, loser.

Aloud she said, "Sleeping," and yawned to prove it. Wouldn't he just go away? She shoved the bag into her dilapidated tote without looking inside. She'd throw it out later, couldn't stand thinking of his hands all over it.

He seemed unwilling to leave, and she had to press against the window to avoid contact.

"Thanks again," she said.

"Guess I should go back to my seat . . ."

"Guess so."

"Unless you'd like company . . ."

"No, thanks."

Did other women have such trouble being heard? Did men think because she was *Indian* she'd be game for anything? Seemed to her she made herself clear. Why wouldn't they take "no" for an answer?

On the other hand, she was good at losing those she loved.

Of her own people, her younger sister Teresa was the only one to do more than stop over a few hours to say hello. Even Teresa visited only once, not long before Marty came on the scene.

The best thing about Teresa's visit was having someone to come home to. Emily didn't take her sister to all-night parties, but sometimes they went on double dates, even though Teresa had a "kind of" boyfriend back home, someone who wanted to marry her and have babies with her.

"So, what do you want?" Emily had asked.

Teresa said she wasn't sure; she'd come to the city to find out.

If Teresa had found a job, a lot of things might have been different. She told Emily she clammed up during interviews, figured people would think she was just a dumb Indian anyway. How would *they* know she'd gotten all A's in her grade twelve departmentals?

"Because you tell them," Emily would say, giving Teresa a little shake. She liked playing big sister. "Or you get Mom to send your report card. You must have your report card . . . ."

"It's lost. You know how it is. Can't keep track of anything around there."

Poor Teresa

Finally, Emily gave up trying to help. She and her sister were very different, maybe because Teresa hadn't needed to fight for things. Teresa had stayed home and behaved herself, while Emily had broken the rules.

Kicked out.

Emily sometimes wondered if her mom regretted sending her first-born daughter away. With all the others to worry about, maybe Emily had just slipped from her mind. Meanwhile, Teresa *belonged*, and Emily had to hide how jealous that made her. Fortunately, Teresa was so sweet it was hard to resent her for long.

Emily also knew her sister tried not to be a burden. Besides looking after the apartment and making meals, she went for long walks or to the public library. After a few weeks, Teresa knew more about old "Pile O' Bones" than Emily had after five years in the city.

The double dates were Emily's attempt to show her sister a good time while also protecting Teresa and her own reputation. All Emily's careful planning was wasted, however, when Teresa's date, the buddy of Emily's current boyfriend, tried to get into Teresa's pants.

When they had pulled into the parking lot for the drive-in movie, Emily tilted the rearview mirror to keep watch on the backseat. Before long, however, she had problems of her own. Like most of the Greek guys Emily knew, Antonis was cute and always pushed the limits. He'd start with the arm looped over the shoulder, kissing her nice enough, gently rubbing her sleeve. Then he'd want her to unbutton her coat, and before long his hand was inside her blouse, forcing her to prove she was serious.

It was a familiar game, and Emily knew both rules and benefits. This time she had responsibilities; otherwise she sometimes let Tony win.

She'd just evaded more of Tony's fondling when she happened to glance in the mirror and couldn't see Teresa at all. Sure enough, when she twisted around to check things out, Teresa was flat on her back, with Tony's buddy — whose name was Stavros — sprawled on top of her, his hands way out of bounds.

Stavros returned to his corner pretty fast when Emily slugged him with her purse. Teresa sat up and pulled her skirt back over her knees without meeting her sister's eyes. At least she hadn't lost her underwear.

Emily wanted out of the car and would have dragged Teresa with her, but Tony said "don't be *vlakas*." (She'd heard that before and knew he meant "stupid.") Tony also said he wouldn't let them freeze, and they could keep it anyway if they was so fussy. To be on the safe side, Emily made her sister move up front beside her and told Stavros he was lucky she didn't have a knife. If they were treated like squaws, they might as well act the part.

"*Putanas, oloi putanas*," muttered Stavros, and being called a whore didn't surprise Emily either.

The next morning, as Emily was buttoning herself into her receptionist uniform, Teresa stood in the bedroom doorway and told her sister she thought she was ready to go home, that she didn't like the city after all. Emily felt the now familiar stab of jealousy. If that fella back home liked her sister as much as she'd said, what did it matter if Teresa couldn't make it in the city?

Lucky Teresa.

Emily via the Greyhound Bus

On her own again, Emily considered following Teresa back to the reserve. According to law, it was also her home. If only she knew she'd be welcome. Their mother had a new man — a good man with kids of his own, Teresa had said. The house would be full. After awhile Emily stopped imagining it was possible.

Keeping Up with Her Reputation

WHAT HAPPENED TO EMILY HAD HAPPENED to others, but for her it changed everything. The invitation to come home never arrived. She did get presents: packages of Kookum's bannock, some of her mom's old books — she'd gone to a convent school as well — a pair of moccasins. When her kookum died, it was her mom who wrote to tell her. By the time Teresa came to visit, the moccasins were the only thing from home Emily had left. Books were too heavy to carry from place to place.

At school she had discovered a blank stare protected her when she felt threatened, and she had learned to smoke, since it was forbidden. To her surprise, she was popular. The other girls said she was beautiful, with her dark eyes and glossy black hair. They were fascinated that she had "done it" — the story of her baby had spread in spite of the sisters' attempts to contain it.

Not that Emily had told anyone. You just can't hide some things. Emily did tell stories of her early life, usually embellishing the truth, since the girls expected it.

Served them right.

"What was it like?" they asked, their eyes bright.

Emily knew what they meant — something she hadn't wanted to remember, much less speak of. When the girls persisted, she made it sound romantic. After all, their worlds revolved around clothes, makeup, and guys. What guys said, looked, did. How they kissed, touched, tried to touch; whether there'd be a letter, when they'd see them again, whether to go all the way next time they saw them.

Since there was no privacy, everyone knew when hearts were broken or someone was bitchy because of her period. Emily found much of this ridiculous, in spite of liking the attention that came her way. It seemed that the nuns weren't the real power in the school, though no one wanted to be the girl caught misbehaving. Emily hadn't heard of physical punishment; the disapproval and loss of privileges were weighty enough. Parents seldom turned up — and for Emily, never. Popularity with the other girls was everything, which meant taking risks.

So peer pressure drove Emily out when she was seventeen. She left to prove she could, though the other girls admired her and the sisters said she had adapted well. Some of the nuns even seemed to like her. Why shouldn't they, when she was a quick learner and neat and orderly in appearance?

Yet Emily had to live up to her reputation, and running away was easier than she expected. One night she simply packed her clothes, her makeup, and a few mementos from the other girls and crept into the silent hallway. It was after "Compline" and lights out, so most of the nuns were tucked away in their tiny rooms in the other wing of the building. The halls weren't guarded and the dorm rooms not locked, in case the girls needed the washroom overnight. There would be a night Sister reading under a desk lamp somewhere; however, rigid discipline was against the House Mother's principles. "Trust is more important than policing," she would say.

All Emily's dorm mates were cheering her along, some lying awake, listening to her tiptoe along the long hallway and down the broad oak staircase. Out the two sets of heavy doors to the chilly night air and the freedom it promised — whether she sought it or not.

Even as she left, Emily had regrets about letting the sisters down. Her math teacher, Sister Elizabeth, had said Emily could probably go to university on a scholarship. That conversation came back to Emily in the months that followed. Another favourite was Sister Virginia — so odd looking in her horn-rimmed glasses, her long black robe and veil — with such a serious gaze Emily had felt the Sister was seeing right through her. Years later, Emily thought about writing Sister Virginia to say she was sorry. As if a nun, so separate from the real world, could understand!

It hadn't taken Emily long to find a job and a place. For a pretty young woman, waitressing jobs didn't depend on a grade twelve diploma. She kept in touch with her school friends for awhile, until other companions filled their places. The attention from men was a heady thing, but she played her cards with care. She knew there were two types — those going somewhere and those who weren't, and she wasn't wasting time on the wrong kind. Neither was she getting into trouble again. Hadn't they just invented a pill to keep you from getting pregnant?

Emily awoke to the crackling of the intercom.

"Now arriving in Thunder Bay. If this is your destination, claim your luggage at the side of the bus. For those continuing to Winnipeg and beyond, this will be your lunch stop, re-boarding begins in thirty-five minutes.

"Please leave some article of clothing et cetera to mark your seat, as we will be boarding additional passengers. There will be a change of drivers, so make sure to have your ticket with you."

(Polite cough)

"I hope you enjoy the rest of your journey. Thank you for travelling Greyhound."

Emily via the Greyhound Bus

The bus slowed, made two right-angle turns, and ground to a stop in the protesting snow and gravel of the parking lot.

To Emily, the idea of lunch wasn't appealing, but she supposed fresh air might help. Oddly, she craved a cigarette, when she hadn't smoked since Marty had made her quit. Funny how he'd turned out to be so health conscious and middle class.

The cafeteria attached to the Thunder Bay Greyhound station was a barn of a place, yet had the essentials — a clean and roomy Ladies, a new lunch counter, and lots of tables. Once in the lineup, Emily realized she was ravenous and ordered a hot beef sandwich, apple pie, and chocolate milkshake. When the sandwich finally arrived, with its steamy mounds of potatoes, gravy, and bright green peas, she balanced her tray as she paid, then found an empty table in a corner.

It must be obvious she was travelling alone, and she hated being conspicuous. She'd learned to ignore being ogled but also disliked being patronized and having to make conversation with strangers. And she was so out of practice at being single.

Jeremy . . .

There had been a bad moment when she saw the pay phone by the door; fortunately, she hadn't enough change for long distance and couldn't call collect, not after the things he'd said. Neither was she sure how long the twenties she'd taken from his wallet would last.

Emily had scarcely started on her sandwich when the call came to re-board. She looked down at her plate.

Too late for take-out now.

All she could do was grab some serviettes from the well-thumbed dispenser. The sandwich made a soggy package, and the apple pie was almost as bad, even on its paper plate. Damn it, she wasn't about to leave food behind.

She managed to gulp down her milkshake and swallow most of her peas and mashed potatoes. Would she make it to her seat without another half-hour visit to the can? Why had she thought she was so hungry!

The new driver was buckled in and adjusting the mirrors when she climbed aboard, holding up her ticket like a shield. To her surprise, he merely grinned and closed the door behind her.

That's okay, then.

Winning and Losing

WHEN EMILY REACHED HER SEAT, A stout, white-haired woman was installed in her place. Much good it had done to leave her tote bag to reserve her spot! She'd been taught to respect her elders — maybe it didn't count if they weren't Native. Besides, she knew how this type proved their charity by "chatting" non-stop and thrusting countless snapshots of fair-haired grandchildren under her nose. She'd have to be ruthless.

"I'm sorry, ma'am," she said, leaning close and managing to slur her words. "Need a seat to myself. Upset stomach. The runs. You don't wanna be sittin' next to me."

For a moment, it seemed the older woman might argue; finally, she grabbed her packages and jostled past. There were other spaces nearby, not that Emily cared. When she'd dropped her soggy sandwich and pie into her shoulder bag, she established her territory further by wrapping her coat around her like a blanket and pretending to be asleep.

Before long, she wasn't pretending. Might have slept peacefully if Marty hadn't intruded again. Thoughts of him never made for pleasant dreams.

Before she met Marty, Emily linked up with people in the oddest places, not just at parties, but in laundromats, waiting rooms, and downtown cafes. He, on the other hand, looked as if he'd never been in a laundromat, much less made his social contacts there.

It hadn't taken him long to get high, and then he was caressing Emily's breasts through her peasant blouse. Nor were they the only couple making out in the fragrant, smoky room. When a more private space was necessary, they found a well-worn mattress in a back room. The next morning, they made it back to Emily's apartment, and Marty showed no sign of ever wanting to leave.

Too good to be true. Thought I'd dreamed him.

Emily later discovered Marty wanted a cause and wondered what a low life he thought her, since he enjoyed saving her so much. However, it wasn't her role as the maiden in distress that did her in. It was the times he didn't seem to be playing a part, like at Aaron's birth. He'd insisted on being in the delivery room, where he held her hand and panted and pushed along with her. And when he kissed their newborn, he kissed her blood-smeared belly as well, almost as if he were about to go down on her right there, in front of everyone — like some kind of holy pledge.

"My woman," he said, his eyes luminous. Behind him were the surprised faces of the doctor and nurses, yet only Marty was in focus. The moment seemed to last forever, and she loosened whatever restraint had protected her until then and let him break her heart. For, even as he put his brand on her there in the delivery room, Marty was beginning to leave her, and it had taken all these years to heal.

And now Jeremy was gone as well.

How can I bear it?

When Emily opened her eyes again, she was cold, disoriented, and aching all over. Her coat was a crumpled heap on the floor and her skirt twisted around her. Worse, the fellow from outside the toilet had claimed a seat directly across the aisle. He smirked as she caught his eye, and she suspected he'd had a pretty choice view as she slept.

She barely resisted giving him the finger. Couldn't he take a hint?

She dragged her coat up from the floor. It was black suede leather, one of the few nice things she had and a present from Jeremy last Christmas. They were still okay last Christmas.

Then again, maybe not.

As she draped the heavy folds around her, she regretted her rush to escape, wished she'd packed, grabbed a pillow, found a sweater, changed into jeans. In a skirt, one so easily ended up looking rumpled and sluttish. At the time, however, she'd obeyed an overwhelming urge to punish Jeremy and forget how she'd let him — and herself — down. Now, she just wanted to hide.

"Buy you supper, Miss?"

"Uh . . . no," she hesitated a second too long, and the fellow seemed about to slide in beside her. She stared him off.

"I'll see how you feel about it later."

Just you try, bud.

She watched his broad back as he ambled toward the front door. He'd combed his hair and put on a good-looking jacket. Too stocky to be her type, though that kind of bulk was comforting. What was she thinking! Nighttime always made a wimp of her. Where were they? Dryden? Kenora? Perhaps she should cash in her Cross-Canada Pass and pick a destination. But where?

"Has that fellow been bothering you, Miss?"

She started. Now the bus driver was standing over her. She hadn't noticed his height before or the hair that reminded her of Glen Campbell on those old record covers. One of the girls at school had had a crush on Glen Campbell.

"Nothing I can't handle."

She'd used that line a lot in the past.

"Call on me if you need to. By the way, this is a meal stop. I'll be turning off the engine and closing the door. It'll be — he looked at his watch — forty minutes before we start up again. Might get pretty cold."

Emily thought about the mushy remains of her lunch somewhere at the bottom of her bag. "You mean I can't stay here?" she asked.

"You're not supposed to; however, I can't see the harm, if you're sure . . ."

"I'll be fine," her face split into an answering grin.

"Okay then — and remember, when we're back on the road, I'm up front if you need me."

Comforted, Emily curled up under her coat again in the empty bus. Jeremy had once made her feel safe and warm as well. However, it wasn't Jeremy who pushed his way back into her thoughts. When their "honeymoon period" was over, Marty never let her feel good for long.

For many years, Emily had had a recurring nightmare. First, Marty's kiss on her belly and his mouth rising up marked with her blood, as if he'd been sucking the life out of her. Then she'd notice Dorothy, his mother, standing in the wings.

While Emily lay helpless, Marty would take their dark-eyed boy–child away, ignoring the fact the cord anchored mother and child together. Moving in slow motion, he would place the child in Dorothy's arms. The cord would stretch thin and fragile as cobweb, without letting go, and Emily would feel something inside her being torn away as Aaron and his grandmother disappeared into the shadows. Before Marty too floated away, he gave Emily another tender, grateful kiss.

In reality, it took much longer for Marty to disappear and take Aaron with him. It took two years of the grime and misunder-standings that made up their daily existence — not any kind of life for a hero.

Emily via the Greyhound Bus

It took a court case and cross-examinations. Marty used everything he knew about her against her — even the way they met. In the courtroom, everyone was against her. Besides, she believed the verdict. How could a woman who had drifted for so long be fit to raise a child?

He was going to love me forever.

Hero with Feet of Clay

BECAUSE THE END OF THE LOVE affair with Marty cost her so much, recalling the beginning was like remembering someone else's life. Not long after Marty's parents met Emily, they offered Marty what he called a "walkabout" — an extended holiday in Europe or Australia. Though he took the money, Marty told Emily it was a bribe to break off with her. Emily was hurt and indignant, even if his honesty seemed to prove his loyalty. Nothing, it seemed, could make him betray her.

Instead of taking the trip, Marty bought a farmyard — the surrounding land belonged to a real farmer. The farmyard boasted a ramshackle house close enough to the city for Emily to drive to work, while Marty worked on his novel. The house was really a one-room shack without running water; it had electricity, a furnace, and an outhouse — all Marty felt they needed. Since Emily had grown up in a house with no bathroom, she'd have sacrificed much more to support her man.

They were two against the world, with their bed the centre of their universe. Neither of them was the least bit handy; any time they attempted to fix something, they made it worse, so they didn't try anymore. Kettles leaked, cups had lost their handles, and floorboards creaked under linoleum worn black on all the traffic areas.

Cracked windowpanes let in both heat and cold or were repaired with once-white adhesive tape now turned gray. The place also had that cloying smell of mice because both the wooden siding and the cement foundation anchoring it to the ground were riddled with cracks and holes. And, since both Marty and Emily loved the earth too much to kill any living creature, what ventured inside was smart enough to stay. Usually this attitude didn't create any problems. Until one morning Marty had woken up first and headed for the outhouse. Suddenly he was in a rage, and Emily gazed at him in groggy disbelief, uncertain what was wrong.

Then she too saw the butter dish. It had been abandoned on the table overnight, and a scattering of mouse droppings showed where visitors had feasted. Normally they'd both have laughed at the black trail of appreciation.

It was Emily's first glimpse of Marty's anger, even though he raged at his parents often enough. He went to the door and hurled the offending butter, dish and all, into the old caragana hedge that pointed the way through knee-high grass to the outhouse.

"Nobody can live like this!" he hissed.

There was obviously more to this than just a butter dish. When he started to open and slam cupboard doors, she got up and went to comfort him — and reassure herself.

He shook her off. And Emily, who thought herself tough as leather, was suddenly tissue paper thin. She went back to bed and stayed there most of the day, first to grieve and then to be comforted by a repentant Marty.

But it was only the beginning.

The day in bed meant a second day of work missed — on the first, they had celebrated her pregnancy — and before long she had lost another job. Not much of a job — waitress and barmaid at a highway motel on the fringe of the city — but necessary, since it bought their groceries. Marty's novel wasn't finished, so it would be a long time before a publisher hunted it down.

Fortunately, Marty's parents had forgiven him for spending their "blood money" and might help them further. Nothing would be forthcoming from Emily's parents. Her father had died long before Emily left home. As for Tanyss Maurait, Emily's mom, just because her life was better now she had a new man didn't mean Emily could ask for a handout.

One of the few times Emily had seen her mom since leaving home was when Tanyss and Samuel Maurait were invited to the home of Marty's parents. It had been Marty's idea. He and Emily had been together a few months, and he was fascinated by some idea of going Native.

Though Emily hadn't thought the visit such a hot idea, she generally went along with Marty's schemes. And maybe she wanted to show off a little. "My man's got money; I must be somebody." That fancy house said it all.

Talk about a fool!

The evening was a disaster, as it was bound to be. Emily scarcely spoke to her mom, for within half an hour Tanyss quietly took offense and walked out of the Feldstein's elegant Queen Anne home on Leopold Crescent.

The crisis occurred because Martin Sr. came home late from work and hadn't been prepped by his wife. Dorothy was finishing up in the kitchen, and Martin started mixing martinis. Poor fellow, he was only doing his hostly duty, as he would have done for any dinner guests.

So, when his wife came through the swinging door from the kitchen, Martin was about to serve Natives hard alcohol. Dorothy didn't say anything; she just shook her head and gave a telling glance at the tray of drinks. Tanyss intercepted the glance and read its meaning correctly.

Emily via the Greyhound Bus

With a dignity that belied her shyness and ill-fitting Fortrel pantsuit, Emily's mother rose up from the tightly stuffed French Provincial settee and announced she wouldn't be staying for supper after all.

Her new mate looked disappointed. A preview of their meal was wafting from the kitchen, and Emily doubted her family had many opportunities to sample roast beef and Yorkshire pudding. As for the promised English trifle — with or without brandy — would her mom have known such a thing existed? Yet Samuel wouldn't leave his woman to find her own way home.

Sam did the right thing.

As far as Emily could see, her stepfather seemed to believe all men were brothers and his life enriched by the differences between them. Still, if he had to choose between these people and his wife, he knew his priorities.

When Emily thought back on the sorry little episode, she wished she'd followed Sam's lead. Instead, she'd been trying to prove she was good enough for the Feldsteins and was ashamed of the woman sitting like a dumpy Fortrel pigeon in that oh-so-tasteful living room. First being reluctant to take off her threadbare coat — then that suit! Emily had turned her back on her mom as if unable to stop herself.

Stupid, stupid, stupid.

Long before the coach door reopened and the first passengers began to re-board, Emily regretted staying on the bus. Her coat wasn't intended to be a blanket and was getting crumpled and dirty from dragging on the floor.

Wreck everything I touch.

So when the fellow from across the aisle appeared again, bringing coffee — it would have been tough to refuse his company.

Besides, his obvious attempts to impress were rather touching. Maybe it was only conversation he wanted. What point was there being rude when she was cold, tired, and lonely?

So he sat beside her and talked practically all the way to Kenora. Told her his name was Clifford — Cliff for short — that he'd been living in Red Deer. He'd just visited his parents in North Bay and was headed to Fort McMurray, hoping for a job in the oilfields, since he'd heard there was no end of opportunities there. She only half listened. Still, she got out with him at the next coffee stop, waited around while he had a cigarette, and let him buy her coffee and a muffin. She owed him something for distracting her for almost two hours.

When the bus was loading again, Cliff took it for granted they would continue sharing a seat. Fortunately, he dozed off when he found she'd stopped listening.

After a while, she started to doze again too, and back came Marty.

The custody battle — which she'd lost before it started — had happened in earnest when Aaron was about three years old. They had put her on the stand and asked her questions.

"How old were you during your first pregnancy? . . . What kind of mother gives her baby away to strangers?"

"How can you provide for your child? Have you ever kept a job for more than a few months? Have you any support systems you can turn to?"

"Do you wish to deprive your child of the benefits the Feldsteins can offer?"

They kept on at her until Emily quit fighting. How could she explain? Could she tell them how Marty had called her his woman, like it was a sacred bond?

Only in a few things had Emily ever resisted Marty. After the episode of the butter dish, she dreamed about mice and about bugs infesting tender baby flesh and became obsessed with getting away to some place clean and safe. So it was she who suggested they take up the Feldstein's offer to stay with them, at least for a few months. Of course, she hadn't been safe there either.

Marty, who had enjoyed her "earthiness," suddenly became scornful of everything that came naturally to her — such as walking barefoot. Later she suspected the changes started with his mother. Though both used her pregnancy to excuse their "concern," there seemed to be more to it. Did they think she might revert to something disgusting if they didn't watch her constantly?

What Marty's father thought of her, Emily never knew. Martin Feldstein Sr. was one of those men whose business acumen was balanced by his desire to let his wife take charge on the domestic front. The "blood money" had no doubt been Dorothy's idea.

Homesick

THE HEAVY HAND ON HER THIGH brought Emily back to the present.

"That must be some dream," said Cliff, his tobacco breath tickling her ear. Emily cursed herself for letting her guard down.

"Take your hand off my leg," she said — no reason to be polite anymore. "I guess you've forgotten where your seat is?"

He pulled back as if genuinely hurt.

"Why so unfriendly all of a sudden?" he wanted to know. As he fumbled his way into tight cowboy boots and struggled to his feet, she almost felt sorry for him; not that she'd relent.

"I guess you'll tell me when you're in the mood for company again."

Not likely, loser.

Cliff made a production of getting settled again across the aisle, where the man who had taken over his earlier spot wasn't any too happy about sharing. Served him right, thinking a muffin and a cup of coffee was the price of a feel.

Emily rearranged her coat and bag, remembering the trouble sympathy had caused her in the past. Like when she was thirteen and raped behind the barn. Her cousin Travis had caught her during a game of tag and dragged her through the underbrush. Her ankle was wrenched and her back scraped and bruised, but she was so naïve she didn't know the game was finished until her panties were torn and blue jeans down around her ankles. Then she felt his weight pressing her open, followed by another kind of tearing and the trickle of blood on her thighs.

Later, he sobbed on her shoulder for all his griefs and begged her not to tell her parents. Everyone knew her father's temper — the family, the elders, the public health nurse — so she hid what had happened. The blood she could wash away; hiding the bruises was more difficult, since she and her sisters shared a bed.

Worst of all, she had known Travis watched her, his strange eyes glowing from his thin, dark, secret face. She had admired the way his wind-blown black hair hung over the collar of his denim jacket. If it weren't for her vanity, she could have been the good girl her mother wanted. Instead, she had been slinky as a cat, tossing her head and letting her bottom sway when she walked.

Innocent or not that first time, there was no excuse for walking with him again, for walks always ended in neighbours' barns, sheds, burned-out cars, or dark patches of bush. She didn't know whether she was more afraid of Travis — for he was often angry — or of coyotes and the other stealthy creatures of the night. Yet she never refused to go with him. Wasn't this mixture of fear and yearning part of being a woman?

That winter her father died. Cirrhosis of the liver, the doctors said. If Travis hadn't been her cousin, the secrecy could then have ended. In the old days, many girls became wives when they were very young. But living so close was dangerous, and their family believed a cousin was almost a brother.

Sometimes they kissed and petted as they lay down together, and one of those gentler times her cousin Travis gave her a baby. She knew when because a few days later he left the reserve and went north into the deep bush with her Uncle Emile, her mother's brother, who followed the trap lines. Emily never saw either of them again.

Her kookum was first to see the changes in Emily and to read what they meant. Her mom slapped her eldest daughter's face, though she'd never hit one of her kids before.

It wasn't my fault!

"Foolish girl," Mom said. "You were s'posed to finish school and have a better life than me, maybe come back and be a teacher. Now, you've got to leave."

"No." Emily was sick with terror. "You need me. I can help with the little ones."

Tanyss, however, was unrelenting. "I have Kookum to help. You think I want all my girls to end up with a baby like you?"

So Emily knew she was a bad example to her sisters and could have died of shame. Mom's voice softened.

"You know what happened to me when I came back and had you? Fifteen years and never a kind word from your old man. You want to end up with a face like this?"

Emily saw the small white scar that spoiled the shape of Mom's mouth and another scar above one eyebrow. But she wasn't persuaded.

"I can't go and be with strangers."

"The sisters will look after you better'n me."

The sisters did look after Emily. However, no one comforted her when she cried for her mom and her kookum in the middle of the night, or during the worst pain she'd ever known. It wasn't that the sisters were cruel; rather, they seemed afraid to touch.

When this new pain was finally over, they told her it was best she didn't see the baby. She only knew she'd had a boy because she overheard a conversation.

"Small, of course — poor thing's only a child herself — yet a fighter. He'll have to be," said one who was a nurse.

"Look at all that hair," said the other. "They're such beauties at this age."

Though she couldn't hold her baby, Emily secretly gave him the name "Fighter." Later, the sisters said the agency had found him a good home, though Emily never learned where or with whom. Doubtless some clean-living couple took her baby and raised him *almost* like he was their own.

My little Fighter.

Alone in the darkness, Emily had to admit she'd made some mistakes. But babies themselves weren't mistakes, and wasn't the greater sin taking them away? Why did other people always think they knew what was best for her?

The sisters, Jeremy, Marty and the Feldsteins, all the fast-talking lawyers and judges, maybe even her mom. They'd taken too much from her — even when trying to protect her. A baby makes a girl a woman like a man makes a girl a woman. If that baby or that man is taken, a wound keeps bleeding just like milk kept seeping from her breasts and staining her school uniform when she was fifteen years old and they took Fighter away.

This was the wound that always needed to be filled, the one Jeremy couldn't understand. How long, in fact, had it taken her to understand?

The Verdict Was Self-defense

IF JEREMY HAD MEANT WHAT HE said about loving her and wanting to know her, it was already too late. When she stuffed a few things in her shoulder bag and slammed out of his house, the old Jeremy was already gone.

Emily dared not think about that either. The list of thoughts to avoid got longer and longer: first Marty, then Jeremy, and — always — the sons she'd lost. And here she was, reminding herself that she was alone because she had to be.

She looked outside and saw only snow, plus a few trees craggy and alone-looking against a blue black sky. They were past the rocks and forest now, and she'd forgotten the bleak look of a prairie winter.

Inside wasn't much better — only the dim glow of a few reading lights held back the dark. That fellow Cliff seemed to have moved to the rear of the bus again. She dared not check, in case he saw her and took it as encouragement.

A couple of seats forward, there was a sleeping child. Nine or ten, she figured, noting his shaggy dark head hanging over the armrest. He twisted in his sleep, trying to get more comfortable, thrusting one knobby, denim-clad leg into the aisle, head drooping further, mouth gaping open. Only a child could bend in all directions like that, all fear and resistance lost in sleep.

Once she too must have been that young and trusting, if she could only remember when. There was also something familiar about this child.

Fighter?

Either of her sons might look like him. Or might have once; both were older now. Fighter would be mid-twenties — maybe with his own kids. Even Aaron could be a father. Though, with the Feldsteins in charge, he'd more likely be getting an education or doing a walkabout. Not starting a family.

Odd to imagine her son travelling the world, mixing with big shots like a rich boy should. And here was she, riding the Greyhound bus, no money and no home. She'd hate him to see her like this. Tears brimmed up again, and she searched her coat pockets for a Kleenex. Since when was she so weepy? She'd been alone before. Yet the tears came. In a minute she'd be bawling out loud, with everyone on the bus pretending not to hear.

What the hell, they'd just think she was drunk, especially if she had to go to the toilet for tissues. Besides, after all these hours on the road, the toilet would stink and make her sick again.

About then the bus lurched to another stop. No wonder they called this the "milk run." The stop brought the driver to mind. Earlier, she'd admired his helpfulness to everyone and how he made her feel safe. Now she noticed the western cut of his jacket and the fact his trousers didn't pull tight across his backside. Too sure of himself to show it off, though she could tell he was well built. His stomach was lean, his legs long, and there was a pleasant curve to his behind.

The darkness allowed her to watch more closely, even when he came down the aisle to count passengers and tap wayward feet aside. Once he seemed to pause beside Emily, his waist at about eye level, so she dared not look up to meet his eyes or look down, although she felt a flutter of excitement.

Too bad about the haircut; it reminded her of singles' dances. She'd met too many single guys after the Feldsteins took Aaron — one could get used up. Lonely men. Clean-cut cops, mailmen, and accountants, fresh out of marriage, with something to prove. In the end, they never wanted what they thought and settled instead for what they'd left behind. If she'd played the game a little smarter, by now she might have someone who'd never leave her.

Jeremy.

Jeremy had been different. That's why she'd followed him to Toronto.

"I'm not going to disappear on you," he had said when she'd told him the hard facts of her life. So for twelve years they'd slept together, cooked together, planned together, looked after each other.

When had he begun shutting his office door, working evenings, suggesting she get a place of her own? Was it because he wanted her to take charge of her life? Or was he trying to get out of his promise?

Again the voice over the intercom interrupted her.

"We're arriving in Winnipeg. There will be a change of coaches and a forty-minute stop for those going on to Brandon, Moosomin, Whitewood, Regina, et cetera. If properly marked, your luggage will be transferred. If this is your destination, please claim your luggage at the side of the coach."

The vehicle rounded the corner and waited for the barbed wire security gate to open. Then it went over the hump into the parking garage.

Boy Did I Get a Wrong Number!

WITH NO REASON TO HURRY, EMILY stayed in her seat after the other passengers — even the youngster ahead, who was nudged awake by a girl who could have been either sister or mother — had climbed down, dragging knapsacks and potato chip bags along with them. Cliff had pushed by her without stopping, and then the Glen Campbell haircut came within a few inches of brushing her cheek.

"This is the end of my run," he said. "Is someone meeting you, or can I buy you a late supper?"

She gazed wordlessly at him for a moment.

"I have to check something first," she said, pulling her coat around her shoulders and picking up her bags. She needed change for the telephone.

Careful not to look back, Emily strolled down the aisle. If he wanted to catch her, it shouldn't be difficult since it was awkward clutching her coat with one hand and lugging her bags with the other. She had almost reached the door when he called out.

"Name's Larry," he said. "I wind down at the Salisbury House. If you don't see me, ask. Somebody will know."

An uncomplicated guy with a manly look about him, a guy who made her feel sexy as well as safe. So why was she playing hard to get? Why the phone call when Jeremy's position was perfectly clear? Why should he forgive her? He wasn't the one who'd put their relationship at risk by going to bars and pretending to be available. Maybe, after twelve years of living together, she owed him a call.

She headed for the ticket counter, imagining either the window closed or agents grouchy. When she was younger, she'd enjoyed giving back as good as she got. Now, unpleasantness just made her feel worthless.

Two or three dollars worth should connect her to Toronto. And, if Jeremy wanted to know, it should give her time to tell him that she was okay.

If he cared.

"Excuse me, sir. I'm sorry to trouble you, but I wonder if my ticket's still good."

Why was she apologizing? No matter how tough she got, how classy she tried to look, her voice still sounded like somebody asking for a handout. Were some things hidden so deep you could never get free of them?

Marty had hated that. "No wonder you women get abused," he'd said.

Damn Marty.

"Let me see what you have there, Miss," said the agent, extending his hand. He even smiled. "That'll take you all the way to Vancouver just fine," he said, "or any place between. Just show it to the driver when you get on. If you're going west, there's a forty-minute wait before the last bus. Better not miss it. Unless you've got some place to stay."

"Thanks — oh, could I get change? I have to phone home. Toronto."

Why did she tell him all that?

Even after Emily started to dial, she wasn't sure about calling. What if Jeremy wasn't there? Or hung up on her? What if he never wanted to see her again? What he had said was he needed someone he could trust, who could pull her weight. When she was doing her best. Yet how could she argue?

By the time he answered, Emily had convinced herself he wouldn't be there. She heard the operator's voice as well and the rattle of the coins in the metal slot. They seemed to take forever.

"Emily, is that you?"

"Hello, Jeremy."

She'd always liked the feel of his name in her mouth, soft as the skin at the back of his neck. Remembered how he used to hold her for no particular reason. Their bodies swaying together — like you can't help rocking when you're holding a baby.

"Where the hell are you?"

"Winnipeg."

"Why Winnipeg? You don't have anybody there."

"I just took the bus."

"Are you alone?"

Emily understood what he meant — had she run off with someone or picked up someone along the way? How dare he? She knew the answer.

"Emily," his voice was gentler. "Are you all right? Do you have enough money? You didn't even take your suitcase."

"I'm all right," she managed.

The operator's voice cut in then, and Emily was out of change. She thought she heard Jeremy say, "call me when you know where you're going," yet wasn't sure.

The dial tone cut him off, leaving her bereft, coat slipping off one shoulder, tote bag crammed into the shelf beside the phone, half the contents of her purse — comb, lipstick, wallet, keys — spread out in front of her.

Emily hung up and scraped her belongings into her purse. She wanted to rest her head on the shelf beside the phone. She wanted to sink to the floor, sink into the floor, disappear — that'd be better still.

Most of all, she wanted to stop caring and knew if she stayed in one place the pain would return. There was only one way to make it better.

Three minutes later, Emily stood at the entrance to the Salisbury House. It was easy to pick out grey pant legs and shoulders, an overnight case on the floor. Larry and one or two other drivers sat in a red plastic booth near the kitchen. Laughing and shooting the breeze as if nothing could touch them. Though she knew enough about men to realize it was generally an act, it still looked good.

Emily strode directly across the room and was beside them before they knew she was coming. "May I take your order, gentlemen?" she asked in her sexiest hostess voice.

Three male faces looked up at her, half-smiling, unsure. Then Larry stood, gave her a courtly little nod and offered her the place beside him. She took her time, tossed her hair out of her eyes.

"I'm Jack," the younger of the two across the table greeted her as he sat down again.

"Emily," she extended her hand, pretending not to notice his was wet with perspiration. Because he looked as if he might say something foolish, she turned to the man beside him.

A tougher customer, she could tell, smiling too, but sitting easy in his seat, taking her measure. He picked up his cigarettes, didn't even ask her permission.

It was Larry who thought to ask. "Do you mind if we smoke?"

She hadn't expected him to be a smoker — maybe something to do with the late hours. Why come across like a spoilsport, however? They were here first.

"I'll be getting along anyways," said the older man. He looked at her more kindly. "Nice to meet you, Emily. My old lady knows the time my bus gets in, gets ticked off if I don't show up pretty quick."

The younger fellow hadn't noticed the lay of the land and offered to buy her coffee.

"I've got that covered," said Larry. "Thanks anyway, Jack."

Emily relaxed against the plastic seat.

Jack finally got the message. "I'm off," he said.

Larry reached across the table to give him a pat on the arm.

"See you next week, bud. Oh, and send Geraldine this way. Tell her we need coffee and menus."

When the waitress arrived, Larry called her "Geri." She was young, fresh faced and spoke as if she were a student.

Girls like Geri made Emily uncomfortable. Though Jeremy had encouraged her to get her degree, the smarts she'd learned at university never rested easily on her. She always felt she was going to be found out, while girls like Geri were born to it.

Ordinary men, though, she could handle. And she wasn't getting overlooked because of a pretty waitress. Her shoulder rubbed Larry's as she shrugged off her coat, and he leapt up to hang her precious leather on the hook at the end of the booth.

Geri asked if they'd like to order, and Emily tried to remember how many twenties she had left — only two, she thought. She shook her head.

She felt Larry's hand clasp her knee.

"I'll look after this," he said and ordered Salisbury steaks with all the trimmings. Emily felt more tension fade away.

Her mind ran ahead. There'd be a taxi to his apartment — much better than a hotel room — and pawing each other in the elevator. How well she knew the scene.

"What about the photos of your kids you promised?" Geri was asking.

After a slight pause, Larry answered, "They're right here."

Out came the envelope. He didn't look at Emily, and over his shoulder she could see two sandy-haired youngsters in jogging suits.

Emily knew what was coming next.

"And your wife?" asked Geri.

There was the tall, fair-haired woman smiling into the camera like she'd never known an anxious day in her life.

"I'm going to miss my bus," said Emily.

She pushed her way out and grabbed her coat, wincing at the sound of fabric tearing. When she was almost at the entrance, someone touched her arm. Geri handed her the shoulder bag. Her expression was rueful.

"Sorry," she said. "Some guys get away with too much."

"Piss off," said Emily.

Stranded

EMILY MADE IT TO THE GATE as the "Now Loading" sign came off its hook. The attendant glanced at her ticket, mumbled "might be out of luck," and hustled her through the doorway. Then, while she hammered on the door of the coach, the attendant tried to catch the driver's eye. By the time the door opened, Emily's knuckles were sore. Again there was something satisfying about physical pain. Almost as good as cursing or screaming.

The new driver wasn't pleased to be held up and insisted on opening the luggage compartment for her, though she assured him she had no luggage. Eventually, he allowed her inside, and soon Emily was huddled in another seat, coat over her, bag under her head. Just about the time she decided she'd be awake for the rest of the night, she must have fallen asleep, for the driver was announcing a ten-minute smoke break at Moosomin.

Her watch said 4:20 AM as the bus pulled in beside the Esso station with the sign saying "Open 24 hours." Emily felt numb, stiff, and nauseated, so she stumbled toward the back of the bus. Would she even make it this time?

Though the sign said "Occupied," she too rattled the door latch. No response. She turned and floundered to the front of the coach — almost fell down the steps. Her canvas shoes gave no protection against the snow and ice, yet she managed to stay upright until she made it past the pumps and into the shadow of a storage shed.

At that point, she focused on wasting on the ground the little she'd eaten that day and scarcely noticed the cold. When she stopped heaving, the faint heat rising from her own vomit fanned her face, and she'd have been sick again if there'd been anything left to lose. Alone, broke, and empty, she wished she were dead.

"Stand up straight. Look strong, and that's what the world's gonna see. No help to show how bad you're feeling," that's what Kookum would say.

Emily didn't care. Jeremy didn't want her, and other men only wanted her for a night at a time. What was left to be strong for?

A few minutes later, Emily took in fully that she was wearing only a skirt and T-shirt. About the same time, she noticed the Greyhound pulling out. Leaving her behind. She'd found her patch of privacy all right, and — with all except the most dedicated smokers asleep — nobody would notice she was gone.

She raced for the lighted area, slipped and fell heavily against a pile of cement blocks half-hidden in the snow. More bruises — if anybody cared. When she was on her feet again and into the light, the bus was well down the highway. She stood there coatless, with empty hands, and watched it fade into the distance.

"Life sucks and then you die." That'd been one of Marty's favourite quips, and she'd once wondered how he could joke about it.

At least the shock of watching the bus leave without her had cleared her head. Obviously, she wasn't ready to die quite yet.

She dashed to the service door, where the teen-aged attendant looked up from his magazine.

"Where'd you come from?" he asked conversationally.

Emily could hardly form the words.

"The bus left without me," she managed.

"Guess you'll have to catch the next one. Comes about ten in the morning."

Something else dawned on Emily. Fortunately, she'd used up her quota of crying for this trip. She'd hate to bawl in front of this pimply kid.

"M-my purse and ticket are on that bus," she stammered, her chin shaking from the cold. "I can't even buy a cup of coffee."

"Gee," said the attendant.

"I don't suppose . . ." Emily began.

"Lemme talk to Lil," said the boy. He left her and the counter unattended, disappearing through the door that said "Restaurant." Emily smelled sausages and eggs through the swinging door and felt woozy again.

She found a chair under the bubble gum and peanut dispensers, sat down, and leaned her head forward until it was hanging over her knees. A huge pair of running shoes appeared in front of her — the kid again.

"Lil says go ahead in and have your coffee. She's alone out front this time of night."

A few customers looked up as Emily entered. Truckers probably, refueling their bellies as well as their machines. Lil had to be the one in the yellow smock. She was doing refills of coffee and approached Emily in a businesslike manner.

"You the one missed the bus?"

Emily nodded.

"And left your purse and everything behind you?"

Emily nodded again.

"You better sit down over here. I'm about to make a new batch of coffee."

"What you have is fine."

"You'll be sorry. It's the bottom of the pot."

She led Emily to what was apparently the staff booth.

"So why'd you leave your stuff behind? Some of us love our smokes but not that much."

"I-I don't smoke. I was going to — to throw up — didn't have time . . ."

Lil sat down across from her. "Got the flu? Or are you pregnant maybe?"

Pregnant? Emily stared back at her. That was one thing she hadn't worried about since she'd been with Jeremy. Something about a low sperm count, him having mumps as a child. After she threw out her birth control pills, they used the rhythm method — more or less — and in twelve years had never been caught.

"You look like you've seen a ghost. Not that bad, you know. I've been through it four times. Three practically grown and now a two year old. My old man almost fainted when I told him. He said sixty's too old to be somebody's pop. Wouldn't change a thing now."

Emily scarcely noticed as Lil was called over to another table. Was it possible?

Her Own Kind

WHEN LIL CAME BACK WITH FRESH coffee, she brought a sweater. It gave off such a whiff of smoke and cooking grease that Emily almost lost it again. Soon, however, she was grateful for the cardigan's knubby warmth draped about her shoulders.

Before too long, the warmth, well-sugared coffee and Lil's good-natured chatter were putting Emily to sleep. She hated to be rude — the woman obviously enjoyed an audience.

"Hey, sweetheart, got some time for a regular customer?"

The deep, quietly teasing male voice startled Emily from her doze. A man she'd never seen stood beside them, yet she recognized something about him. She looked away as he leaned over Lil.

"It's okay," said Lil, pushing him away. "This is my old man. Somehow he always happens along when I'm working night shift. Where's the kid?"

"Wha'd'ya think? Asleep in his bed, just like his sisters."

"I thought they were sleeping over."

"On a school night! No way, so your babysitter's ready to roar." Emily blushed again as the man nuzzled Lil's neck.

She also felt that jolt of envy.

"Go on, you," said Lil. "You keep my friend Emily comp'ny while I get back to work."

Emily started to protest.

"Joseph," the man extended his hand. "I'm pleased to meet you, young lady. Are you staying here in town or travellin' through?"

"I guess I'm travelling through."

"Where you from?"

It had been years since Emily had said the name aloud: "Okanawey."

"You kidding me? I got people at Okanawey. I'm Indian too, you know."

"Yeah, I can tell. I got eyes."

"And a smart-ass tongue for a young thing talking to her elders. You live there or visiting? You don't look like a country gal, so you must be from the city."

"Just visiting."

Again, Emily had surprised herself. This gray-haired man with his gravelly voice and face like corrugated wood was having an odd effect on her.

"Gotta go to the can," she blurted.

"Sister," he put out his hand as she slid from the booth. "You don't have to be scared of me."

That's when she started to bawl in earnest.

When Emily finally came back, the booth where they'd been sitting was empty. She avoided Lil's look of motherly concern.

"Don't you worry about Joe," said Lil. "He didn't mean to offend you. He's just real used to young folks coming to him when they're in trouble. All kinds of young folks. He's an elder, you know."

"He seems like a good man," Emily managed. She wished she could explain what had come over her. Almost like coming home after being away for a long, long time.

Lil slid in beside her and put an arm around her shoulders. Emily smelled kitchen grease, smoke, Yardley perfume and something else. The something else was familiar too. When Emily shifted uneasily, Lil took her arm away.

"I hope I didn't offend *him*," said Emily.

"Lord, no. He had to get back home. Now he's checked on me, everybody's accounted for. He'll sleep 'til morning, then turn up at the end of my shift."

"So I'll see him again?"

"I guess so, since the bus comes about ten, and my shift's over at seven. Unless you're planning on disappearing before that . . . "

Emily smiled in spite of herself. As if she would wander into the cold with practically nothing on twice in one night!

Lil stood up. "I just remembered," she said. "There's a couch in the office next door. If you want a lie down, I could wake you before I leave."

For the last hour and a half, Emily had forgotten her immediate situation. Now panic hit again.

"I don't know what to do," she said.

"Nothing you can do. Depot in Regina's closed 'til six. Might as well get some sleep."

When Emily didn't move, Lil said, "You got to trust people sometime. If I was going to leave you high and dry, wouldn't I have done it already?"

Emily nodded sheepishly and soon followed Lil to the room behind the service counter. The decor consisted of a desk and chair, both piled with greasy-looking papers, and a sagging couch. Over the back of this makeshift bed was a homemade afghan of the same vintage as the furniture. All in all, the best proposition Emily'd had in a long time.

She could hardly wait until Lil was gone before curling up under the afghan and closing her eyes.

True to her word, Lil woke her in good time.

"Think you can manage breakfast?" she asked. "So you don't have to tell your story to the next shift."

Emily accepted gratefully and was treated to a full meal as well as ginger-chamomile tea and a take-out bag of soda crackers.

"Did wonders for me last time I was pregnant," she said. "Imagine working the morning shift — all those food smells — wanting to up-chuck every minute."

Emily was getting used to the idea of a baby, though it'd be another thing when she was back on the road going nowhere. Only once had Jeremy seemed to mind not having children.

He'd been scowling into the bathroom mirror. "Why don't you get yourself another man? Don't you want to be a mother, for God's sake?"

It wasn't the time to remind him she'd already lost two babies so wasn't concerned about biological clocks. Much good having babies had done her in the past! As for the rest, sure he was fifteen years older, yet his fine-boned good looks and shaggy gray locks still caught the eyes of other women.

There was only one language she knew to comfort him, so she kneeled and made love to him right there as he stood before the mirror.

Later it was hard to believe such a thing had been said.

What she depended on was his presence — his arms, his chest, his warmth, his hands cupping her head. If only this baby — if there were one — could have happened at any other time in the last twelve years!

By the time Emily was having her second cup of tea, it was the end of Lil's shift. She'd just taken off her apron and slid in the booth when Joseph appeared, moving in that quiet way Emily remembered.

Her father had moved like that, and there was something of her cousin Travis as well. The first two men she'd loved. In spite of the beast her father became when he drank, the way she and the others had to hide from him; and how her cousin hurt her and left without saying goodbye — she still felt their loss.

After all, she'd known their gentleness too. When she was little, her father's hands seemed big and safe, cupping hers, lifting her up whenever she fell in the process of stumbling after him.

Because she was the first of his children, he'd taken her walking in the bush. He'd taught her to see the twigs and branches, how they grew, and to hurry without losing sight of the world around her. He showed her how to find the killdeer's nest in the long grass and watch the nestlings without frightening the parent birds away. He even showed her the gems in the little creek, magic stones that hid their colours when she stole them from the water.

When Emily was old enough to go walking by herself, she brought back to her father the treasures she'd found. Once she discovered a dead bird, its body so light, with brittle twig feet sticking in the air, perfect feathery head sunk into its still soft breast, and she had cradled it from the creek to the house. Her father told her about death, how the spirit leaves the body, and showed her how to place the body with respect and mark the spot.

Before long, however, there were too many children to feed and no game to hunt or fish in the river. When the government money came, there was always a party. When it was gone, the drinking started in earnest.

She'd almost forgotten what it was like before all of them, even her mom, were afraid of her father. Somehow this stranger, Joseph, made her remember.

In the end, drink killed Emily's father. And, because there was so much pain, none of his people could be with him in the hospital when he was dying. Emily had wondered how his spirit could find its way home with no friends or family there to show respect to his body. If there was a funeral, she had no memory of it.

By that time, her thoughts were already full of her cousin Travis, and she was giving him the devotion she'd once reserved for her father. Until Travis too went away from her. Everyone always went away from her.

Going Home

"HOW ARE YOU, YOUNG LADY? NOT still mad, I hope."

The voice that reminded her of her dad also brought her back to the present. Emily shook her head.

They were watching her — him and Lil — Joseph with his arm around his wife's shoulders, Lil looking over the brim of her coffee cup and sipping carefully, as if it were still hot. Emily figured they must be anxious to go.

"I'm fine. You don't have to wait." Emily hadn't much practice being grateful to people and wasn't very good at it.

"Is there a bus to Okanawey? Got anybody to phone?"

That was Joseph. Emily shook her head. "Going to the city first," she said.

"Damn, I forgot," Lil snapped her fingers. "We need to phone Greyhound."

She led Emily back to the office, where she searched among scraps of paper stuck on pegs until she found the number she wanted and handed it to Emily.

"But . . ." said Emily.

"Worry about paying when you've some money."

The voice at the Regina depot was surprisingly brisk for early in the morning.

"Yes, ma'am, the Winnipeg driver turned in a purse and bag . . . and a leather coat. They were ready for lost and found when we opened this morning. So we phoned first thing."

"Phoned?"

"Your husband's real worried."

"Husband?"

"Your I.D. was in your purse. So we phoned. You'd better get in touch real soon or he'll be calling the RCMP. Thinks you're lost or kidnapped or something."

So Jeremy *was* worried.

"You there, ma'am?"

"I don't have my ticket."

"Don't worry about a thing. There's another coach in from Winnipeg this morning — be where you are at ten o'clock. I'll let the driver know."

Again Emily struggled over her thanks.

"Just glad we found you, Mrs. And don't forget to phone your husband."

Emily put the receiver back in its cradle. Returning to the restaurant, she found Lil and Joseph about to leave.

"Sure you'll be all right here?" asked Lil. "I told Darlene to give you more tea. You could come out to our place for a couple of hours."

"I'll be fine," said Emily.

Joseph gave her his business card with its geometric drawing in the corner. She read "Joseph Morrisette, First Nations elder and guide, Moose Mountain Medicine Wheel."

He shrugged modestly. "This here's Indian country too. Town named for an Indian chief caught in the middle during the Rebellion — Mounties on one side, Riel on the other. But he wouldn't take sides, only wanted peace."

"Moosomin . . ." murmured Emily. Seemed like she'd heard that story before.

Lil pulled Joseph's sleeve.

"Time we were getting along. Be here all morning if you get started, and one of these days the school bus won't wait for our Sharleen. Besides, I bet we hear from our friend Emily again."

"Thanks for everything," said Emily. So they expected to hear from her? Much had changed in the last few hours. Too much too fast. Maybe that was her problem. She always rushed in before she knew where she was going.

From her booth by the window, Emily watched Joseph and Lil drive away in their eight-seater van. Being an Indian guide must be profitable if they could afford a vehicle like that. Lil wouldn't make much waitressing. The van would also transport tourists. As Joseph had said, this was Indian country.

Hidden beyond that flat prairie were rolling hills and valleys — sacred places, like the medicine wheel on Joseph's card. During the summer, carloads of people would want to explore those places, even if they didn't understand the meaning. And in the backcountry alongside the provincial park, roads were few. Not likely such tenderfoots were up to travelling miles of rolling country with only horses beneath them.

Emily's dad had once owned a horse or two. Of course, she'd been a city girl so long now she'd be as helpless on horseback as the tourists.

Joseph seemed like the kind of man who'd keep horses but be adaptable too. Like her mom's new mate.

Imagine — comparing Joseph to her father *and* to the man who'd taken her father's place! If only her dad had been so lucky, or so smart. Joseph must be right into this stuff about reclaiming your Native heritage — even made a living at it. Maybe Sam was into it, too. With his easy-going manner, he'd make a good elder and ambassador.

When had she last felt compassion for her father? Too bad he'd never seen people like this, making their living without pretending to be white. She'd sometimes thought he died because he didn't know how to be anything but an Indian, in a world that had no use for Indians anymore. She'd even thought she was the same — would have to find her way among strangers or die trying.

Could she go back to being Indian (or "Native" or "Aboriginal" — whatever they were calling themselves these days) — and survive? Not waiting for handouts but doing something for herself? Could she be a teacher like Mom always wanted? Was she smart enough, strong enough? Could she do it on her own?

Could she maybe even find her boys?

When tears started to run down her face again, she didn't try to hide them. She'd a right to cry over her lost children, men born of her own body. And over all those other men she'd lost. Screw these friends of Lil's if they couldn't handle a few tears in their restaurant.

It didn't seem, however, that the two waitresses, Darlene and Angela, were paying Emily much attention. They were too busy with paying customers to notice a stranger crying into her ginger tea.

Nine o'clock was obviously the height of the breakfast rush. A charter had just arrived — probably from the States. She heard the accents and saw them clustered in their too-heavy parkas. Like they'd expected Arctic not prairies — and all the tables were jammed.

Emily couldn't handle any more tea, so there wasn't much to do except watch the two women swish back and forth in their yellow uniforms and soft-soled shoes. They were like nurses, like they'd never wanted to do anything else.

If Emily couldn't be a teacher, maybe she could find a little highway place to run by herself, with a cook or another waitress to help in the summer. Live in the back with her baby. Why not?

Because of Jeremy?

She should phone him — didn't need the police looking for her, that's for sure. Why was she was putting it off? Jeremy had said she needed him too much. Maybe it was him who needed her.

Where would he fit in this new life she was dreaming for herself? Would she be the mother of his child for a couple of years only to see his love die for good as Marty's had? Would he ever think she was good enough? One thing was sure. If there was a baby, she wasn't giving it up, whatever she had to do to keep it.

There seemed to be no help for it. Jeremy would have to wait until she was ready, and she'd have to wait and see about him. Whether when the time came he'd be willing to come to her, or whether he'd still be making excuses.

She wasn't just thinking about what was best for her baby. She'd lost too much of herself, and no one had loved her enough to make up for that loss. Maybe she was the one who thought she wasn't good enough. She'd have to fix that before she could feel safe with any man. Able to believe that happiness couldn't just disappear in a puff of smoke if she said the wrong thing, made some little mistake.

She'd never know if she didn't try it on her own. Not like when she was seventeen. Running away from school just to keep up with her reputation had been stupid. Even then she was looking for approval. What she needed was to be okay on her own. And someday, when she was ready to risk loving a man again, Jeremy might be waiting.

So Emily phoned him and made him understand that she didn't want to see him just yet. She didn't mention anything about a baby. First, she'd have to find out for sure; plus she didn't want to stack the deck. She did promise to phone again when she got to Okanawey — if she could find a phone somewhere. The way it used to be, you just never knew. And who knows how much had changed in twenty-five years.

As she talked to the man who'd been her lover for almost half that time, Emily made herself another promise. Never again would she stay when she was an outsider to the man she loved. Better to be alone.

After she said goodbye to Jeremy, she returned to the warm leatherette of her booth until the Regina-bound coach arrived at 10:05. At 10:15, she was back on the Greyhound bus, with Lil's sweater and the afghan from the office couch wrapped around her.

So the road passed under her, the winter landscape hurried past, and she was on her way into the future. And in her womb, the child nestled — almost invisible now, but growing — infinitely trusting and — because she would make it so — secure.